The Big Race

ALL ABOUT SAFETY

Written by Kirsten Hall

Illustrated by Bev Luedecke

children's press®

A Division of Scholastic Inc.
New York Toronto London Auckland Sydney
Mexico City New Delhi Hong Kong
Danbury, Connecticut

About the Author

Kirsten Hall, formerly an early-childhood teacher,
is a children's book editor in New York City. She has been
writing books for children since she was thirteen years old
and now has over sixty titles in print.

About the Illustrator

Bev Luedecke enjoys life and nature in Colorado.
Her sparkling personality and artistic flair are reflected in her
creation of Beastieville, a world filled with lovable Beasties
that are sure to delight children of all ages.

Library of Congress Cataloging-in-Publication Data

Hall, Kirsten.
The big race : all about safety / written by Kirsten Hall; illustrated by Bev Luedecke.
    p. cm. — (Beastieville)
  Summary: When the Beasties have a race just for fun, a series of accidents may mean the
winner is not the fastest one.
  ISBN 0-516-23671-7 (lib. bdg.)   0-516-25517-7 (pbk.)
  [1. Racing—Fiction. 2. Accidents—Fiction. 3. Stories in rhyme.] I. Luedecke, Bev, ill. II. Title.
  PZ8.3.H146Bht 2004
  [E]—dc22
                                                            2004000127

1 2 3 4 5 6 7 8 9 10 R 13 12 11 10 09 08 07 06 05 04

EAS
A NOTE TO PARENTS AND TEACHERS

Welcome to the world of the Beasties, where learning is FUN. In each of the charming stories in this series, the Beasties deal with character traits that every child can identify with. Each story reinforces appropriate concept skills for kinder-gartners and first graders, while simultaneously encouraging problem-solving skills. Following are just a few of the ways that you can help children get the most from this delightful series.

Stories to be read and enjoyed

Encourage children to read the stories aloud. The rhyming verses make them fun to read. Then ask them to think about alternate solutions to some of the prob-lems that the Beasties have faced or to imagine alternative endings. Invite chil-dren to think about what they would have done if they were in the story and to recall similar things that have happened to them.

Activities reinforce the learning experience

The activities at the end of the books offer a way for children to put their new skills to work. They complement the story and are designed to help children develop specific skills and build confidence. Use these activities to reinforce skills. But don't stop there. Encourage children to find ways to build on these skills during the course of the day.

Learning opportunities are everywhere

Use this book as a starting point for talking about how we use reading skills or math or social studies concepts in everyday life. When we search for a phone number in the telephone book and scan names in alphabetical order or check a list, we are using reading skills. When we keep score at a baseball game or divide a class into even-numbered teams, we are using math.

The more you can help children see that the skills they are learning in school really do have a place in everyday life, the more they will think of learning as something that is part of their lives, not as a chore to be borne. Plus you will be sending the important message that learning is fun.

Madeline Boskey Olsen, Ph.D.
Developmental Psychologist

Bee-Bop

Puddles

Slider

Wilbur

Pip &Zip

Flippet

Pooky

Mr. Rigby

Smudge

We're the Beasties

Toggles

All the Beasties love to play.
All the Beasties love to run.

One day, Bee-Bop had a plan.
"We should have a race for fun!"

"Count us in!" say Zip and Pip.
Toggles says, "Count me in, too!"

All the Beasties want to race.
Zip tells them, "I will beat you!"

That night Puddles rubs her eyes.
She is tired. She must rest!

She must go to bed right now.
Sleep will help her run her best.

Slider rises with the sun.
It is time for him to eat.

He knows he must eat good food.
"I have Zip and Pip to beat!"

Everyone is ready now.
They all line up in a row.

Flippet says "I will be judge!"
She says it is time to go!

Zip and Pip think they will win.
They are passing everyone.

"I love racing, Pip!" says Zip.
"We will win! This will be fun!"

Flippet flies above the group.
She brought water for all ten.

Toggles takes a few small sips.
Now she can run fast again.

Flippet calls out, "Watch the ground!
Look out for that pile of dirt!"

Bee-Bop does not hear in time.
He falls down and says, "That hurt!"

Slider slides down in a hole.
He is moving very fast.

He does not know where he is.
"Now I guess I will be last!"

Smudge is running. He is last.
Poor, big Smudge is very slow.

Smudge tries hard. He is not fast.
"This is as fast as I go!"

Zip and Pip have almost won.
They run fast and they are quick.

Oops! They are not looking down.
They both trip on a big stick.

Here comes Smudge. He wins the race!
"Zip and Pip! Are you okay?"

They both wave back. "Yes, we are!"
Big Smudge wins the race today!

THE RACE

1. How many Beasties are racing?

2. How many Beasties are there in all?

3. How many feet can you count?

SOUNDS LIKE...

"Face" is a word that sounds like "race." Can you think of any other words that sound like "race"?

SAFE RACING

Running is good for the body.
But you have to run safely.

1. How do the Beasties get ready
   for the big race?

2. Which Beastie tries to make sure
   everyone is running safely? How?

3. What happens when the Beasties
   are not racing safely?

WORD LIST

a	falls	know	ready	this
above	fast	knows	rest	time
again	few	last	right	tired
all	flies	line	rises	to
almost	Flippet	look	row	today
and	food	looking	rubs	Toggles
are	for	love	run	too
as	fun	me	running	tries
back	go	moving	say	trip
Beasties	good	must	says	up
be	ground	night	she	us
beat	group	not	should	very
bed	guess	now	sips	want
Bee-Bop	hard	of	sleep	watch
best	has	okay	Slider	water
big	have	on	slides	wave
both	he	one	slow	we
brought	hear	oops	small	where
calls	help	out	Smudge	will
can	her	passing	stick	win
comes	here	pile	sun	wins
count	him	Pip	takes	with
day	hole	plan	tells	won
dirt	hurt	play	ten	yes
does	I	poor	that	you
down	in	Puddles	the	Zip
eat	is	quick	them	
everyone	it	race	they	
eyes	judge	racing	think	